For my dearest grandma.
– Ellen

Dear Grandpa Santo,
I dedicate this book to you.
You didn't keep a diary, but together
we filled page after page of the diary of our lives.
I am proud that those pages are so full of you.
– Ilaria

Copyright © 2021 Clavis Publishing Inc., New York

Visit us on the Web at www.clavis-publishing.com.

Lissy's Diary written by Ellen DeLange and illustrated by Ilaria Zanellato

ISBN 978-1-60537-650-9

This book was printed in July 2021 at Drukarnia Perfekt S. A., ul. Połczyńska 99, 01-303 Warszawa, Poland.

First Edition
10 9 8 7 6 5 4 3 2 1

Written by Ellen DeLange
Illustrated by Ilaria Zanellato

Lissy's Diary

Clavis

NEW YORK

Lissy skips down the sidewalk holding her mother's hand.

They're going to her favorite store to buy presents for Grandma.
It's her birthday!

With the gift nicely wrapped under her arm they walk to
the flower shop next door. Lissy picks a colorful bouquet.
She can't wait to give the presents to Grandma.

Grandma quickly opens the door
when she sees them coming.

"Happy Birthday, Grandma,"
says Lissy, as she gives her a big kiss.

Then Lissy turns around,
"Bye Mom, see you later."

"I'm so happy you're here," says Grandma. Lissy follows her into the kitchen, where it smells delightful.

Lissy carefully brings the teacups into the living room, and Grandma carries the pie.

"We bought presents for you,
Grandma," says Lissy as she
hands her the flowers and
the nicely wrapped package.

"How wonderful! These are my favorite flowers," says Grandma. "And what a beautiful diary, thank you so much!"

Lissy is happy that Grandma likes the presents. She's curious about something though.

"What actually is a diary, Grandma?" she asks.

"Let's eat some pie first," says Grandma.
"Then I'll read to you from one of my old diaries.
I think that's the best way to explain what it's all about."

Lissy is still licking her fingers when Grandma
walks over to the bookshelf.

She's very curious and can hardly wait for Grandma to read from this book called a diary. She curls up on the coach, sitting close to Grandma. Grandma starts reading.

January 15
It already has been freezing for many nights.
I wonder how long it takes before we can go
skating. I will ask Dad tomorrow.

"I love skating too, Grandma," says Lissy.
Grandma smiles and continues reading.

January 16
At breakfast this morning Dad said
that we could go skating this afternoon.

I had a difficult time concentrating in class.
All I could think of was going skating.
After school Dad was already waiting for me
with our skates.

We went over to the pond in the park.
It felt a bit wobbly on the ice at first, but
it didn't take long before I could skate again,
without holding Dad's hand!

After a couple of rounds around the p̶a̶ pond, I heard a strange noise.

I skated over and saw that there was something moving.

It was a duck, stuck in the ice.

When I came closer it frantically flapped
its wings, trying to escape.

I looked around to see where Dad was. He was
busy talking to our neighbor and waved when
he saw me. I knew I had no time to lose,
I had to rescue the duck myself!

I saw a long stick and got an idea.
I grabbed the stick and quickly skated back
to the duck. I carefully poked the ice around
the duck with the end of the stick. I heard
the ice crack. The duck was quiet now.
I wondered if he knew I was trying
to help him?

All of a sudden, the duck flapped its
wings again. It jumped on the ice
and walked away loudly chattering.
I was so happy that it had worked!

Dad was very ~~prowed~~ proud of me when
I told him how I rescued a duck.

"That's so exciting," says Lissy, "I'm so glad that the duck was set free. That was very brave of the little girl. I wish I could do something like that!

Please read on, Grandma! I'd love to hear more."

Grandma flips through the pages and continues reading.

May 10
Today was not a happy day.
This morning everything was
still okay. When I walked back
from school I picked some
wild flowers for Mom.

When I got home I searched
for a vase. The only one
I could find was
high upon a shelf.

I tried to reach it, but when
I thought I got it, the vase
slipped right out of my hands
and fell on the floor.

I was shocked.
Fortunately, only a few pieces had broken off.

I tried to glue the pieces back together as best as I could.
Luckily you could barely notice it any more.
I put the flowers in the vase. It looked so pretty.

But I know I will have to tell Mom about the vase.
I just have to figure out the best moment to tell her.

"Oh oh," says Lissy. "Was her mom upset when she found out?"
"Her mom was a bit sad her vase was broken," says Grandma,
"but she wasn't upset. She was happy that it was glued back together
and she loved the flowers."

Lissy sighs relieved. Fortunately that ended well . . .

"I really would like to hear more stories," says Lissy.
"The girl seems very nice. What's her name?"
"You already know her name," says Grandma.
Lissy looks puzzled. "What is it, Grandma?"

"Her name is Lissy," says Grandma.
"But that's my name," Lissy says surprised.

"The little girl I'm reading about is me," explains Grandma to Lissy.
"And as you know, you're named after me," she says with a big smile.

"I wrote these stories when I was a little older than you are now. Over the years I have kept many diaries. I still write about the things in my life that matter to me, so I can remember them forever.

Would you like to write in a diary as well?" Grandma asks.
"Yes, I would love to," says Lissy. "I think that's a great idea!"

When Lissy's mom picks her up to go home, Lissy can't stop talking about the stories from Grandma's childhood.

That evening Lissy can barely sleep. She's so excited that she'll get her own diary tomorrow.

When school is out,
Grandma waits for her
at the school gate.
Lissy skips over and takes
Grandma's hand.

They walk over to Lissy's
favorite store. Lissy chooses
a journal with beautiful
flowers, white swans, and
ladybugs on the cover.
"Thank you, Grandma,"
she says while giving her
a big hug.

Lissy keeps her new treasure close to her chest when they walk back to her house. She can't wait to write in it. Back home Lissy runs to her room and climbs on the bed.

She opens her diary and starts writing:

Dear Diary,
Today . . . .